# The Story of

# THE WALNUT TREE

To Madison and Miranda Morley, AnnMarie Dearden,
and to the wood experts, Ben, Ben Jr., and Brad Banks.
—DON H. STAHELI

To Vicki for her love and support.
—ROBERT T. BARRETT

Text © 2000 Don H. Staheli

Illustrations © 2000 Robert T. Barrett

Design: Scott Eggers

Bookcraft is a registered trademark of Deseret Book Company.

Visit us at www.deseretbook.com

ISBN 1-57345-885-6

Printed in the United States of America                                                    42316-6766

10 9 8 7 6 5 4

❧ The Story of ❧

# THE
# WALNUT
# TREE

Written by Don H. Staheli

Illustrated by Robert T. Barrett

The first few weeks in April, when the snows have gone and the grass is yellow green—that's the time to plant a tree. And every year, those early April days brought the same kindly man to the plant nursery to fill his cart with saplings. He bought maples, quaking aspens, and evergreens: maples because they grow tall and strong, aspens because they shimmer in the breeze, evergreens because they smell like Christmas.

owever, one April morning, the man did something different. As he planted the new saplings behind his house—the house he had helped build with his own two hands for his wife and children—he stopped to examine a bucket of black-walnut seeds that a neighbor had given him. He had never planted a black walnut before, but something about the idea pleased him. He smiled a thoughtful smile and placed one of the seeds in his pocket.

**T**hen, after planting the saplings, he dug a small hole in the ground with his shovel. He placed the walnut seed in the hole and covered it with soil, patting it down tightly. The man was excited to see what this little seed would become. ❧ He was a busy man, coming and going to meetings, but he always took time for his family, and he always cared for his trees. He pruned them and watered them and pulled the weeds that grew up around their trunks. He worked with his children in the yard and taught them about trees. They were careful not to step on them or hurt them in any way.

As time passed, the little walnut grew, but never as tall or as full as the other trees, it seemed. ❧ The maples grew strong and wide. They scraped the sky with their scalloped leaves. The children thought they were majestic. ❧ The quaking aspens grew beautiful white bark. Their leaves shimmered in the wind—shining green in the summertime and glittering gold in the fall. ❧ The evergreens grew bushy and full. The children could hide away under their boughs and not be seen.

Once, while the kind man was watering his trees, one of the children asked, "Why is the walnut tree so slow to grow? Will it ever be tall or wide or have beautiful leaves like the others?" ❧ The man looked over at the walnut. "Sometimes the things that take the longest to grow turn out the best," he said. ❧ Another child asked, "But what good is the walnut tree? Its branches are too high for climbing. It isn't even pretty like the other trees in our yard." ❧ The man fiddled with the hose. "Often the things that are not so pretty outside are the most beautiful inside," he said. ❧ Another of the children added, "It's not full enough for shade, and it gives us only a few nuts in the fall." ❧ The man stooped down to turn off the spigot. "The best things in life give all they have, even if it isn't very much."

**O**ne spring, many years later when the children had grown up and moved to their own homes and planted their own trees, the walnut grew no nuts at all. Its branches hung low and its leaves did not grow. The kind man could see that the tree was sick. He knew the tree had to be cut down.

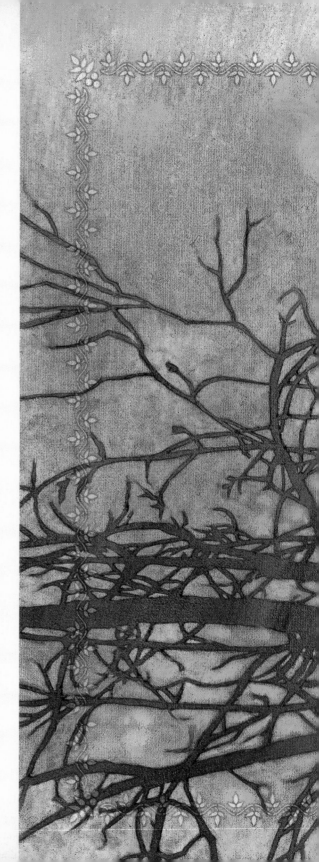

fter so many years of caring for the tree, it made the man sad to think of losing it. But he knew it had to be done. ❧ Knowing the value of walnut wood, the man called a wood expert to see what could be done with the wood from his dying tree. The wood expert had a wonderful idea. He knew of a large building that was being built—a church building. It would need beautiful wood for the walls and for the pulpit where the speakers would stand to give their talks.

Skillful men were finding special trees and using the best wood for the building. They came to the man's house and cut down the walnut tree. They took it to a lumber mill, where the tree was cut into sections. It was then taken to a woodworking shop, where it was dried and shaped into a pulpit. It was lacquered and polished to show the swirls of its grain. When it was finished, it was placed near the front of the great hall in the new church building, where all who came would see it.

Soon many people came to the new building. They were excited because the prophet of the Lord was going to speak to them. As they waited, they admired the beautiful hall and its walnut wood pulpit. ❧ When the prophet entered the great hall, all the people rose to their feet. He was the one they were waiting for. It was President Gordon B. Hinckley, the prophet of God.

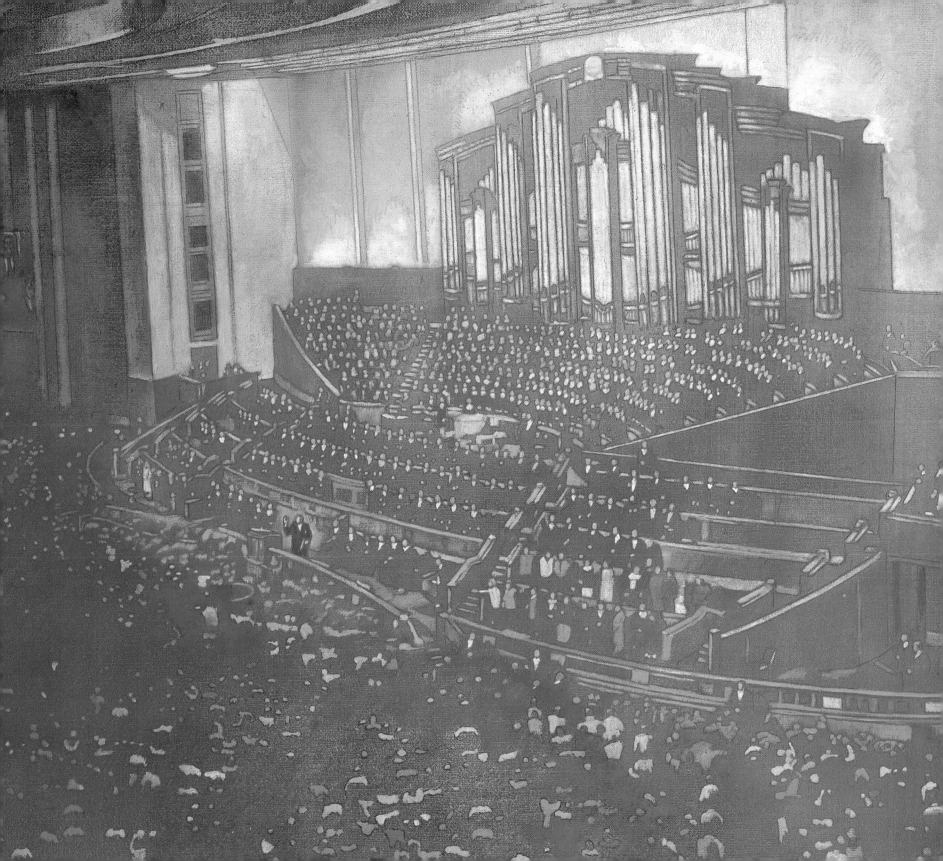

ater, when he spoke from the walnut wood pulpit, the prophet taught the people to obey the commandments and to serve one another. He bore testimony of the Redeemer of the world. Then, rubbing his hands along the grain of the pulpit, he told them about the wonderful little tree from whose wood the pulpit had been built. "I am speaking to you," he said, "from the tree I grew in my backyard, where my children played and also grew." It was he who had planted the little walnut seed so many years before. He was the man who had cared for it for so long.

**T**he walnut tree had taken a long time to grow. It never grew tall or wide like the maples. It never shimmered in the sun like the aspens. It never smelled of Christmas like the evergreens. But now, the beauty on the inside was plain for everyone to see.

And every year, during the wondrous first week of April, when the snows have gone and the grass is yellow green, and later, too, in October, before the snows return, thousands of people would look upon the walnut tree and listen to the prophet speak the word of the Lord.

# RELATED SCRIPTURES

# 1. Sometimes the things that take the longest to grow turn out best.

## ❧ ALMA 32:33-36 ❧

And now, behold, because ye have tried the experiment, and planted the seed, and it swelleth and sprouteth, and beginneth to grow, ye must needs know that the seed is good.

And now, behold, is your knowledge perfect? Yea, your knowledge is perfect in that thing, and your faith is dormant; and this because you know, for ye know that the word hath swelled your souls, and ye also know that it hath sprouted up, that your understanding doth begin to be enlightened, and your mind doth begin to expand.

O then, is not this real? I say unto you, Yea, because it is light; and whatsoever is light, is good, because it is discernible, therefore ye must know that it is good; and now behold, after ye have tasted this light is your knowledge perfect?

Behold I say unto you, Nay; neither must ye lay aside your faith, for ye have only exercised your faith to plant the seed that ye might try the experiment to know if the seed was good.

# 2. Some things that are not pretty on the outside are the most beautiful on the inside.

## ❧ ISAIAH 53: 2-3 ❧

For he shall grow up before him as a tender plant, and as a root out of a dry ground: he hath no form nor comeliness; and when we shall see him, there is no beauty that we should desire him.

He is despised and rejected of men; a man of sorrows, and acquainted with grief: and we hid as it were our faces from him; he was despised, and we esteemed him not.

## 3. The best things give all they have, even if it isn't very much.

And Jesus sat over against the treasury, and beheld how the people cast money into the treasury: and many that were rich cast in much.

And there came a certain poor widow, and she threw in two mites, which make a farthing.

And he called unto him his disciples, and saith unto them, Verily I say unto you, That this poor widow hath cast more in, than all they which have cast into the treasury:

For all they did cast in of their abundance; but she of her want did cast in all that she had, even all her living.

## 4. We love the most those things we work hardest to help.

No man can serve two masters: for either he will hate the one, and love the other; or else he will hold to the one, and despise the other. Ye cannot serve God and mammon.

Wherefore, I give unto them a commandment, saying thus: Thou shalt love the Lord thy God with all thy heart, with all thy might, mind, and strength; and in the name of Jesus Christ thou shalt serve him.

✂ MOSIAH 4:15 ✂

But ye will teach [your children] to walk in the ways of truth and soberness; ye will teach them to love one another, and to serve one another.

## 5. Sometimes things that are old are still very useful and valuable.

✂ JOB 12:12 ✂

With the ancient is wisdom; and in length of days understanding.

✂ MOSIAH 10:10 ✂

And it came to pass that we did go up to battle against the Lamanites; and I, even I, in my old age, did go up to battle against the Lamanites. And it came to pass that we did go up in the strength of the Lord to battle.